The Horror Writers Association Presents

POETRY SHOWCASE VOLUME IV

Edited by
DAVID E. COWEN

Horror Writers
ASSOCIATION

2017

Horror Writers Association Presents Poetry Showcase Volume IV

First Edition

978-0-9858089-7-6

Contents

A Note from the Editor   1
Comments from the Jurors   4
Mirror Madness   8
My Little Green Secret   9
The Apocalyptic Mannequin   11
Night of Tears   13
Salisbury Twilight   15
Stranded   16
A Bad Romance   17
After the End, Before the Dead   18
Atoms and the Void   20
Cthulhu, Call Your Mother   21
Doll   22
Erato   23
Feeding   24
First, the Tongue   25
He Who Has No Name   26
I Haunt This Place   27
Larry Talbot   29
Love at First Sight   30
Love, the Cruelest Monster   31
Meet the Beetles   32
Mirrored Devourer   34
Murder on The Highway   35
Nodding Into the Twilight   36
Past Suicides   38
Pterodactyls   39
Road Kill Technician   40
Scents Upon A Delta Breeze   42
Serra   43
Skin to Scales   44
Spring's Awakening   45
Stitches   46
The Burial Shroud   47
The Crawling Lesson   48
The Familiar   50
The Length of His Spine   51
The Oak Tree's Shade   53
The Orb   54
The Parasite   55

The Prehistoric Garden 56
The Resurrection of Snow 58
The Square Root of Dying 60
The Tanzler Meditations: On Preserving the Corpse 61
The Thing that Ate You 62
They May Not Tell Tales, but They Do Sing Songs 63
This Is Only the Beginning 64
Undercurrents 66
Unravel 67
Where We Are In Space-Time's Shadows 68
Wings 69
Wraith 70
Yew Berry 71
Juror Biographies 72
Authors' Biographies 74

A Note from the Editor

Poetry is dead. Long live the poetry of the undead!

It would be almost cliché to overly lament the contemporary downfall of poetry in American culture. As the president of one of the largest non-university related poetry groups in the state of Texas, the Gulf Coast Poets (approximately 80 members) for the past five years, I have witnessed the effects of this American ambivalence, if not hostility to modern verse. Audiences diminish like characters in Kiyoshi Kurosawa's iconic, and perhaps prophetic film *Kairo* (2001), leaving poets reading to themselves and empty chairs. Paperbound journals published by academic presses seem intent to explore how far they can isolate the craft of poetry from the common man. Ever haughty in the insistence that poetry should not and cannot connect to a general audience these journals walk the path of economic ruin. The 2012 National Endowment of the Arts Survey on Public Participation in the Arts found only 6.7% of the American population still read poetry. The only major art category less popular than poetry was opera. This is with the proliferation of MFA programs and poetry convocations such as the one I have been honored to preside over these past few years.

This is the fate of mainstream poetry today. And perhaps this pending extinction of modern poetry as Christopher Ingraham reported in the April 24, 2015 *Washington Post* is a self-fulfilling prophecy. The energy of the dwindling few to preserve the art of mainstream poetry is commendable, but we are Canute commanding the waves to cease. The waves ignore us. This is especially when the commands we shout to the foamy brine seem to be diatribes on the faults of the waves. Why would the oceans listen? Why would any American audience listen?

But this is not a dirge to a long lost art. Merely because academic Olympians have isolated themselves does not mean that the art must be shuttered in with them. The key has to be to revisit and rekindle the roots of poetry.

To go back to its beginnings and purpose when poetry was not therapy for self-indulgent pity but story telling. The early works of Western literature were not novels but narrative poems. Sometimes these stories were passed on for generations until poets such as Homer and Virgil fine-tuned them into literary masterpieces. The reign of popularity of the narrative poem shames the modern novel. But as in Neil Gaiman's *American Gods* (William Morrow, 2001), only those gods who still have believers survive oblivion. The task of the contemporary poet is not to complain about their microscopic world but to transform the macrocosm. To recreate the lost audience; turn the dust of faded listeners into mud and mold new life. A new genesis for the art.

I truly believe this is the calling of the so-called genre poet. The mainstay of a "horror" or "dark" or "speculative" poet is the story. We must craft a story in poetical form that will build an audience. Our themes are not just the slashing or rendering of flesh but the transforming of horror into the ultimate artistic analogy of true life. In the "real world" the gods do not intervene in murders, rapes and terroristic attacks. We face the demons of life alone. Horror allows the reader to see the true nature of the human condition – the predator and the victim and those who walk the line between the two. To achieve this we have to avoid cliché and a stubborn insistence of the use of archaic poetical form without pursuing the craft of such forms. We cannot imitate Edgar Alan Poe. We must strive to surpass him.

We must tell a story and as with any short story or novel tell it well. There are no byes or passes for genre. We must strive to craft dark poetry so that it can both connect with readers and withstand literary criticism.

The goal of the HWA was to use the HWA *Poetry Showcase* to both recognize the debt owed by horror writers to poetry and its roots in storytelling and to provide a platform for horror writers to expand their talents. Acceptance in the *Showcase* is not automatic, it is earned. Also, acceptance is not merely "selling a poem," it is being acknowledged in a highly competitive publication as the best the genre has to offer. The competition this year was large and fierce. For the first time I presented the submissions to the judges in "blind jury" form. They did not know who wrote the poems and had to judge them by their content alone.

I am very proud to have been asked to be the editor of this year's *Showcase* for the second year. Our jurors this year are all at the top of their craft. Dr. Michael Collings, Peter Salomon and Lisa Morton brought diversity and insight to the judging process. They took their jobs seriously and I am very satisfied with their decision process. I highly enjoyed working with them on this project.

The three featured by Bruce Boston, Stephanie M. Wytovich and Clay F. Johnson were highly praised by all judges. They reflect the trans-generational universality and relevance of dark poetry.

While we are featuring only three poems this year a brief explanation of why that is the case is warranted. Beyond the three featured poems several were held at such equal value that to feature them as well would have expanded the number of featured poems extensively. A bright line cutoff for the top three rated poems was agreed upon by the judges while recognizing that several other poems were highly rated.

Those poems deserve special mention here. Alessandro Manzetti and Marge Simon's "Night of Tears" beautifully tells the story of Cortes and the horror of his invasion. Ann K. Schwader's "Salisbury Twilight" expertly utilized the villanelle form. Robert Perez's "Stranded" also exemplifies the use of "traditional" verse. These poets can proudly say they were at the top of this volume as well. Their poems stand on their own beyond genre as good poems. For that reason I have created a separate "Special Mention" category for this year's volume.

David E. Cowen, Editor

Comments from the Jurors

Lisa Morton

One of the things I've loved about my involvement with HWA is how much new work in the genre I've been introduced to as a result, with poetry being a particular area of discovery for me. For some reason I made it through all of high school and several college English courses without encountering much poetry. Later in life, as a bookseller, I got a little caught up, reading bits of everything from the Romantics to the Beats to post-Beats like Bukowski, but it took HWA to educate me in how much excellent contemporary horror poetry is out there. While I'm still far from an expert on horror poetry I'm now a confirmed fan, so although I don't pretend to have the qualifications of my fellow judges on this volume, I was excited by the opportunity to read so much fine work. As HWA's current President, I couldn't be prouder of our *Poetry Showcase* series, and I think this current volume continues the high standards of the previous volumes. Thanks to our editor David Cowen, judges Michael Collings and Peter A. Salomon, and all of our wonderful poets. Long live horror poetry!

Peter A. Salomon

This year, as we blindly judged the entrants into the fourth *HWA Horror Poetry Showcase*, it was readily apparent that the art form of poetry, so ancient and venerated, has encompassed a vast canvas of artistic endeavors. From poetry that captured forms and structures that have survived centuries of literature to poems that explored the darkest outer limits of imagination, every entry was a testament to the creativity of the members of the Horror Writers Association. It's been a tremendous pleasure and privilege to be associated with this organization and to have founded this *Showcase* and watched it grow into an international competition with three best-selling volumes of poetry (and counting). I stand in awe of everyone who entered, thank you for sharing your art.

Michael R. Collings

My response to reading and evaluating the submissions for this year's *HWA Showcase* volume is surprise and awe—at the tremendous variety of possibilities implicit in dark poetry, from near-SF through dark fantasy to stark horror. Everything was represented by some of the finest poets in the genre. It was a pleasure to work with them.

Featured Poems

Mirror Madness

I don't look at mirrors
often or for long,
for when I do I always

fasten upon my eyes,
ostensibly windows
to the soul, yet when

I look more closely at
my self looking back,
there is the naked id,

wild and rapacious,
yammering to be free.
And in the background

of this stark insistence,
I see a long prehistory
of claw and need,

a collective memory
of ritual and rapine,
myth and madness,

seething back to
the bloody primeval.
I don't look at mirrors

often or for long,
for when I do, I feel
that I could fall in.

— *Bruce Boston*

My Little Green Secret

An English-style vial of green pigment
Hides inside my piano, ghostly as
Moon-silvered glass, opal-pale like some witch-
Friendly potion—a Victorian skull
Grins back, mercury-soaked top hat
Askew its bone-vanilla head

Within I pretend are witch's reagents:
Storm-purpled nightshade, old monkshood, wolf's bane—
Hecate's *Queen of all Poisons*—
Blood-red bloodroot juice –pudding form–
Milk-silky yellow bell, unpasteurized,
Flakes of witch-curled wormwood bark –cinnamon–
And sprinkles of stone-crushed yew berry seeds

> *Its fragrance stings like a necromantic*
> *Effluvium of root-twisted decay*

But within this oak-corked vial –age-hazed–
Lies no *fleurs du mal*,
No floral bouquet from skeletal leaves
And no cauldron-boiled witchcraft scheme—
But instead, the unhallowed science
Of arsenic-laced *Emerald Green*

> *Her opulent walls are papered with it*
> *The mid-winter damp moistens its poison*

Yet, when finely ground, verdigris pigment
Oven-baked in rustic copper
Becomes an odorless, paste-like glaze:
A cosmetic-inspired *Paris Green*—
My very own inheritance powder

Even better for witch-fever symptoms
Her oozing sores have confounded doctors for months

And though vividly delicious on Victorian-papered walls,
It too can be used for painted smiles and smoke-inspired
eyeshadow dyes

Go on, my darling, smudge a little more
–Just a little more–
To conceal your cancered lips and sleep-deprived eyes.

— *Clay F. Johnson*

The Apocalyptic Mannequin

Inside this pile of broken glass
On the edge of splintered wood,
Call my name against the drip-drop of rain on tin,
To the tune of metal grindings and radiation screams;
Wind me clockwise until I start to breathe,
Scoop out the dust in my macramé lungs,
Help me, I'm dead but I'm dying again,
A tortured corpse amongst this toxic waste:

> *...they named me disappearance*
> *...baptized me, withering,*

Still, between the stones that collect in the pits of my eyes
I wilt to the smell of rot and gun smoke,
Cringe at the sound of human consumption,
The tattoo of my ancestor's serial numbers
Burned into my once-blushed cheeks now stained ashen in their
memory;
Please, paint me in the picture of what was once human
Cast me in flesh, build me of skin of bone
There's death in this camp of dystopian nightmare
A plague house filled with bodies made of dreams:

> *...they stripped me naked*
> *...burned me to plastic.*

— *Stephanie M. Wytovich*

Special Mention

Night of Tears

Tenochtitlan, July 1, 1520

Under a kapok tree with its ghost fruits,
which seems ready to make snowing the summer
Cortés, forced to swallow the sharp gems
of his reign of cactus and butchers priests,
observes the red waters of Texcoco,
the perfect parallel of Tenochtitlan's bridges
and the drift of corpses of his rogue army
whose armors float and sparkle,
turning on themselves, in small circles
making the lake look like a soup of stars.

Doña Marina, with her black braided hair,
two turquoises instead of incisors
and the purple tears of the Llorona on her cheeks,
turns her palms toward the dark sky;
she kneels, just in time to grab
a slice of Spanish intestine
fallen from the beak of a greedy eagle
as it continues to fish pieces of conquistadores,
eyes accustomed to dream of Paradise
and wrinkled and blue ripped out tongues
with still nailed above Catholic blasphemies.

The embankments of the city, splattered with blood
suck the spicy flavor of slaughtered Spanish
while the children, with their yellow painted faces,
phosphorescent as road signs,
stand on the banks and the knees of the Calzadas
to fish with their hemp nets,
strangers' severed arms and hands
still clutching gold jewelry,
chipped rosaries and escaped moths

whose magic dust swirls in the air
in a rhapsody of wings' squamas
already flown away.

Who killed Montezuma sings the thrasher,
but the children are too busy with their task, dark eyes shining.

— *Marge Simon and Alessandro Manzetti*

Salisbury Twilight

The shades of ancient dynasties remain
past sunset as the last midwinter light
scrawls shadow artifacts across this plain.

In life they left no writing to explain
these stones they raised for nameless gods' delight:
the shades of ancient dynasties remain

mysterious as potsherds. Why profane
such sacred ignorance? A blade of night
scrawls shadow artifacts across this plain

& graceless landscape, granting even rain
some incantation all its own. So might
the shades of ancient dynasties remain,

as whispers grown too muted for mundane
perception. Nothing mortal (or not quite)
scrawls shadow artifacts. Across this plain

where one sun dies & one is born again,
survivals such as these seem strangely right.
The shades of ancient dynasties remain
scrawls. Shadow artifacts across this plain.

— Ann K. Schwader

Stranded

Trapped beneath the dome of an hourglass,
sea salt on my lips and ankle deep in sand,
a chronicle of scars counts XIII days passed
wandering alone on this deserted island.

Sea salt on my lips and ankle deep in sand,
I pray to be saved and feed my hope to the fire,
wandering alone on this deserted island
the horizon stretches and the smoke rises higher.

I pray to be saved and feed my hope to the fire
with the gulls endless laughter from overhead.
The horizon stretches and the smoke rises higher
as the shells clamor with the voices of the dead.

With the gulls endless laughter from overhead
I carve XIII deeper into a crooked tree.
As the shells clamor with the voices of the dead
I carve XIII deeper into me.

I carve XIII deeper into a crooked tree,
rearrange the words spelled with collected stone,
I carve XIII deeper into me,
deny the death's head grin of relic bone.

Rearrange the words spelled with collected stone,
a chronicle of scars counts XIII days passed.
Deny the death's head grin of relic bone
trapped beneath the dome of an hourglass.

— *Robert Perez*

Showcase Poems
(Alphabetical by Title)

A Bad Romance

She parts his flesh
With a sigh
And a gush
With a rush
Of lust
In the blood

He screams.

He gives his heart
With a gasp
And a push
With a hush
Of words
In the mouth

He dies.

She takes his gift
With a growl
And a groan
With a moan
Of greed
In the gut

She feasts.

— *Megan Hart*

After the End, Before the Dead

The sky explodes in a waterfall of
Burning light and hellish heat.
Everything crumbles and falls
What once there was, there is no more
The light is dying, that world is dying,
Screaming, pleading, bleeding
As the air fades to endless night

Blood drips off your skin like acid rain
The air is frozen. Your lungs are tight
With staggering steps, you search for safety
But you know there is no such place
Not since the horsemen came
Heralding the beginning of the apocalypse

Mutants stalk the edges of your vision
Grotesque with razor teeth and slime
Wandering the dusty ruins, you wonder
When the end will come for you
You leave a red trail for the flesh eaters
Who scurry over the ruins of humanity

What once was alive, only skeletons remain
What exists now, is not meant for you
The only light is radioactive
Dust from the dead
Flickers over blackened earth
An unnatural acid green
The dust burns your throat and eyes
Like vicious fire

They are close now yet your steps slow
Rabid eyes and melted flesh

They snarl and scream like demented souls
Everything that once was is dead
What remains is a world of death

Death will be your dearest wish
As humanity's remains
Set upon you in bloodthirsty droves

— *Aimee Williams*

Atoms and the Void

"In truth there are only atoms and the void." - Democritus

you know too much

you know of the vast, empty
silences echoing in each
hollow atom

you know of the
forces that push you apart, of
the lonely particles spinning
in quiet solitude

you know of atoms and
you know of the void and
you know of
nothing else

she does not know what
you know

she reaches out—
a hand, a touch, a comfort

you know
it is empty

— *Miriam H. Harrison*

Cthulhu, Call Your Mother

I'm tired of sitting alone in exile on park benches,
watching runny-nosed toddlers eat playground sand,
smacking away tiny dogs who try to hump my leg.
The old women here feed stale bagels to the pigeons,
and they never stop talking. Do you know
how many sons are monsters, according to their mothers?
Ha! These dames don't know the half of it.
As the older kids play chicken on swings and slides
I sigh and wonder why I never see my own grand-spawn.
Why did I have to be the one to give birth to a blind God
who never calls his mother? Who never visits, or even emails.
What, the Eldritch One is too good to set foot in Queens?
Madness is no excuse. It's so treatable now. Every other celebrity
and politician is checking in to clinics these days, hitting talk shows,
bragging about their addictions, their trashed hotel rooms,
their screwed-up kids. You know I don't like to complain,
but it's been eons. Cthulhu my bearded son, sitting up in a cold void,
giggling among the faceless stars . . . Are you warm enough?
Are you eating right? I know you're busy, but would it kill you
to stir your tentacles once a year and send a birthday card?
This coming Saturday I'm making your favorite casserole.
Let me tell you, it's no picnic trying to find human flesh
in the freezer at Trader Joe's. Do your old mother a favor:
Make an effort. Drop in for a little nosh. Dinner's at six.
Just this once, Chaos can wait a little longer.

— *Lenore Hart*

Doll

The uncovered face is
grayed porcelain, worn with abuse,
a concave cheek cracked and splintered,
and above, one eye gone, now a yawning cavity
holding the promise of latent menace,
the remaining eye staring as fixedly
as a sibyl channeling prophecies
of secret horrors
hidden behind a sphynx's grin.

Naked and neutral in gender
save for faint traces of the feminine—
long lashes accentuating the eye and
the faint cherry cast to plumpened lips—
unkempt hair singed and wilted, a wild wreath,
its dirt-smudged and roughly scuffed skin
covered in a warped medley of
blisters and melted patches borne
from aborted offerings to
consuming fires,
unveiled from its makeshift shroud,
a dark totem for the lost children.

Though wordless, it somehow
speaks to her in a language
she imagines sounds like
the familiar music
of her true mother tongue,
sweetly grating the ear like
the songs of knives
cutting through yielding flesh
into solid bone,
or the silent perfection of
soft machines rendered hard
and motionless, no longer
needing to defend
or flee or fear.

— *Allan Rozinski*

Erato

Black ambrosia liquid inspiration
Buried in the dark
Dot to dots of the mind

The ellipses
Spider-webbing down down down
Deep into hidden teats that stalactite into
Dripping black icicles of sustenance

Ink and words
Stories beating bleeding
Bleating from the Muse's manila-thin lips
Leaving paper cuts on my heart
Why do I love thee so?

She whispers
Ringing silence in my ears
Tying my tongue and fingers tightly
Squeezing a drop of inspiration beading falling evaporating

Without warning
She ellipses into ink clots bulging
Breasts and hips and heat and sweat unrestrained
Birthing fluid stories in media res

Enchantress Sorceress Witch
Demon Lover
Tell
Don't show

Why I love thee so

— *K. Scott Forman*

Feeding

Voices fading in
Bewitching her clouded mind
A cold touch on her arm
Threads snaking through her organs
An incubus feeding
The warm drip
Flowing up her arm
Infiltrating calm
Warm fog enveloping
Numbing the snakes
Stopping the feeding
A graceful slide
The voices fading
Deformed body
Once beautiful
Now skeletal
Awakening
The snakes... alive
Feeding
Slithering
Up her spine
Through her brain
Morphine drips
Increasing
Breath slowing
Repulsive pain
Darkness

— *Leadie Jo Flowers*

First, the Tongue

He hugs me—that's all
I want him closer, kissing
Now my stomach roars

Too hungry to wait
I press my mouth to his lips
A feast of his face

Sweet seconds follow
Before the sounds of his screams
Salty skin, release

— *Kathryn E. McGee*

He Who Has No Name

Late in the night the gods sigh
Gently caressing a delicate flame
As lotus blossoms sway in response.
A soft whispered prayer carries across rippled sands
Blasphemy on his lips
As he calls forth life from the sacred Scroll of Osiris.
The forbidden fruit of his heart's desire
Lay ripe and ready – a quivering spirit dissolves into the night:
A midnight ritual disturbed.

Kneeling before the Golden Jackal
The tongue of the irreverent pulled painfully taunt
Slowly cut ragged so the gods are not offended by his cries.
The taste of blood slips down his throat
As new incantations – curses,
Damn his immortal soul.
He is acquiescent with his mortal shell
That in spite of his transgression,
His heart will balance true before Anubis.

The priests bind his feet
Wrapping the linen strips ever up his body
No trinkets, gems, or blessings weaved betwixt.
They fold his arms
Across his chest tightly
Summoning a dying embrace.
The jackal becomes obscured
Fear creeps in
Gripping love's lost heart.

The lid is shut: his breathing is labored, smothered.
Sweat soaks his tight shroud.
Darkness, silence are his companions
Into death.
Alone.

— *By Michele Brittany*

I Haunt This Place

I haunt this place.
This place where I died, this place where I linger.

This is my home.
You think it is yours, but it is not.
I am in the floors, the walls, the beams.
I walk my hallways at night, pacing my world with
gossamer tread and in passing by trouble your sleep.

And time has stopped for me.
I live in an eternal now, an endless gray world
with occasional warmth and light.

You are that light.
I may be ghost to you, but you are a beacon of life to me.
You tread my halls all day and night,
walking by me or passing through me,
and most of you never know I am here.

But some of you feel me.
The sensitive ones.
You feel my cold breath on your neck as I wrap around you,
borrowing your warmth for a time.
You turn around, look for that thing you felt but cannot see.
And you find nothing.

But I am here.
I have always been here.
I will always be here.

You may live here, love here, grow old here,
 but you are just a guest in my walls.
For this house is mine.
It always has been.

It always will be.

And when you are long gone, passed to the light if you are lucky,
or turned to a shade like me if not, I will still be here.
A spectre that walks the halls of my prison, of my life, of my
death.

For I haunt this place.
And while you live within my walls,
I will haunt you...

— *Eric Miller*

Larry Talbot

He saw his death,
In the palm of her hand,
Dread chilled his skin,
A pentacle condemned her,

The gypsy's blood,
Tainted his fate,
He inherited the wolf,
A good man defiled by moonlight,

He begged to be bound,
Tears scorched his soul,
And poisoned his lips,
No chain could hold him,

The silver wolf's head
Saved her from his teeth,
It struck and cut deep,
Neither poem nor death reclaimed him,

A father's sacrifice,
Fashioned from love,
Brought peace to a son,
And banished a beast.

— Naching T. Kassa

Love at First Sight

Her heart burst from her chest
—a xenomorphic egress—
skulked across the sticky bar
to stalk her moony prey.
The organ beat its mating call
—a tachycardic timpani—
his eyes shot over drunken heads, and
she caught them in her outstretched hand.

— *Kerri-Leigh Grady*

Love, the Cruelest Monster

She lived like a razor, cutting through days like flesh.
Leaving permanent scars— She was fatal with a capital F.
I rode shotgun, feeling dangerous, because she had a way
of getting under your skin, growing there like a tumor.
The whisky went down like barbed wire caught in my throat.
My stomach turned and burned, my thoughts were a mile away.
I watched the trees pass, my forehead against the glass.
Cars whipped by, wicked painted blurs crossing my window.
She grabbed my hand. Startled, I turned to look at her,
smiling but afraid all the same. None of this felt real.
Ignoring the sensation, I swept my broken pieces aside—
my aching heart a hollow empty cup thrown to the road.
The car sped through time, the minutes becoming seconds.
Before my eyes, we aged, with me always by her side.
Because the bug never learns—not until it meets a shoe,
squashed beneath the treads. Never bothering a look back.
A cascade of lights erupted—red, then blue, spinning.
I swallowed my heart and convinced her to pull over.
The next moments unfolded in flashes, watching her explain,
the cold rain beating out a hypnotic song upon the hood.
They let her wait in the car, warm air blasting from vents,
and suddenly the engine roared, a tiger coming to life.
Gliding down the street like a snake, lightning crashed.
Wipers swished, followed by several loud bangs. Then pain.
Her head slumped against the wheel, lolled left, and right.
The car spiraled, blood soaking the fibers of her shirt.
An abrupt halt shot me out like bait from a fishing rod.
Reeled back in with a gasp, I felt anything but alive.
My world grew dim upon realizing she'd stopped breathing.
No idea of what came next, I only knew what wouldn't.

— *Kenneth W. Cain*

Meet the Beetles

I live with you just a few precious feet away
your face frozen in agony, twisted from pain.

A final veil and vigil has been planned for today.
What's that? This time you have nothing to say?

Your fists are still curled in still and steady violence.
You said you'd never hit a girl—Your words never made sense.

My face is free from bruises, you were careful of that.
My body was your prisoner—I smiled—my mind was not.

I caught spiders—kept in a jar by the sink.
Feeding them moths and crickets—I learned more at the
museum—much more than you'd think.

I knew which ones were bad, bad for you, but good for me.
My heart raced so fast when I put them between your oily sheets.

It didn't take long until you didn't breathe.
You brought upon your own hell, I left you here to remind me

Why I shouldn't be the one to leave—why should I, indeed!
And who is going to question your signature handing over the
deed?

First came the flies, they flew up your nose.
Then came the larvae, wiggling under your clothes.

Exploding with bugs, some black and some blue,
as a host, you were the life of the party, and a toast, one last time,
between me and you.

Soon your flesh will dissolve into a grey, ugly mush.

Your bones will be buried without any fuss.

The beetles arrive and it's my turn to gloat, turning what's left of
you into mulch and white foam.
The aroma is dank, earthy and foul, and now your face is gone,
along with its scowl.

The room fills with thousands of dark little things.
Like bees to honey, I'm covered in beetles—with wings that
sing.

Little legs tickle me peak to knee.
Finally a part of you hasn't made my everything erupt in a primal
scream.

Then they start biting, our time must end.
Looking for their next meal, off into the air they are sent.

I open the door and they fly through.
Up in the sky, they hover for a moment, like a big black cloud or
two.

I wave and nod and they wait for a bit. I lift my chin and blow
them a kiss.

And then they're all gone, the sun shining through,
And then, like a half-remembered dream, so are you.

— *John Palisano*

Mirrored Devourer

You sneer at this skin you call ugly.
Ashy and dry in winter, shiny and darker in summer.
The kinky hair disgusts you because it won't allow for taming.
It smells like coconut and sun.
Churns your stomach.

What you don't know is the skin didn't always look like this.
I drained it until it darkened in death,
suppressed in oppression,
cried out as it grew closer to midnight.
I sucked the deliverance from the hair so that it crinkled,
trying to escape being devoured.

Metastasizing, emulsifying,
this is what I do.
Until I see another I eat better.
Like you.
From the inside out, I melt your being.
Singed hatred smelling of decay and dying.
Blackening your soul.
Assigning you to dark eternity.

— R. J. Joseph

Murder on The Highway

Is what we call it
when men pull over
in gleaming SUVs and trucks.
Roll down tinted windows,
call the girls,
roaming on foot,
and ask if they want to
work.
And girls get in the bullet-shaped
rides; happy to be sitting,
even if just for a little while.
Zipped away, to
empty lots and fields,
abandoned buildings with rusted chains on doors
like dried blood.
Sometimes, the girls come back.

— *Elsa Carruthers*

Nodding Into the Twilight

The train approaches on the rusted
tracks.

Gray men supporting stooped ash-dusted
backs

in battered rows that line the station
board.

Conductor pulls a harsh impatient
chord

and off they chug through stormy, noxious
waste.

The dead men slumber with unconscious
haste

through vistas of black, burnt, and mangled
trees.

They suffocate within a strangled
breeze

and drown in breathless moonlight rushing
by.

They cannot feel their own blood gushing.
Why

do such men heed the whistle's dying
calls?

They've scraped blind eyes from out their crying

skulls.

They ride into the eldritch, churning
mist

and smoke from sacrifices burning.
Wist-

fully the dull men ride beyond the
veil

and from the distant stars respond the
pale

and silent gods with apathy.

— *Joanna Parypinski*

Past Suicides

Splintered wood
Now damp with dilapidation
Roof tiles sag into a gaping maw
As carrion birds burst forth
Jet-black and half-starved

The acrid reek of death
Pervades the surrounding yard
Some small animal, perhaps
Or something much more profound

It watches in waiting
To wear the skin of stolen children
Missing lockets and lost teeth
These small town folk tales never die
And will keep them coming back for more

And as the winter sun
Sinks low into skeletal trees
The crack of a rifle shot
Rings out across barren fields
And the birds take flight
Once more

— *Benjamin Blake*

Pterodactyls

The pterodactyls of my mind turn in the sky
like hang gliders, flap wings of skin to criss and cross,
drop the anvils of their heads and plummet, then arch
to soar again. Ancient eldritch screeches carry
as I pick my way over dusty, rocky ground
hemmed in by violet mountains. Outsized chicks call
from giant eyries. For everything in this landscape
looms ten times larger than it should, like evolution
in reverse. I hear the cries and see the God-blink
sweep of prodigious shadows like offcuts of night
that, once, were the dripped summer song and shadow-flick
of gardenfuls of blackbirds, thrushes, finches, wrens.

— *Mark Kirkbride*

Road Kill Technician

Road Kill Technician,
cleanser, collector got a nasty-ass, "take-no shit" demeanor,
Fancies himself a corpse-inspector, pipe dream forensic "wanna-be."
Good job for a bone and skull collector, not much left to
taxidermy.

No safety zone or place to call home from civilization's constant
encroachment.
RKT's always alert and in motion, scanning endless miles of
pavement
to find those unfortunately flattened into unrecognizable gore,
having failed to make it clean and unharmed across the hard
asphalt to the other side.
It's his morbid fascination, others shudder at the sight and abhor
it.

RKT hovers near high death rate roads and downtown with his
monster truck
Dripping homemade deer attractant whose recipe's results have
proven more than fantastic.
Tips his official cap in remembrance of Linnaeus, Da Vinci and
Michelangelo,
while sketching out the only local road killed wildlife tree of
phylogeny and taxonomy.

Always quick to turn on his charm, so easy to tap into old
emotional trauma.
Frequent witness to that recurrent commuter drama,
Sexy motorist can't stop crying after leaving "Bambi" on the
roadside dying.

Erectile and in control when he nails a big buck
with protective gear, sanitizing hose and shovel in gloved hand.

Fills up his truck then backs up onto the Animal Mortality
Collection Ramp
at the local rendering plant, again aroused, his pants get damp.

Road Kill,
lucky if fresh, no flies, maggots or foul odors yet,
organic, free-range specialty meats.
Free, feral food, if you so choose and if you're in the mood.

No need to be squeamish, eyes are clear, blood unclotted.
Still has fleas? One can be pleased, it can be your next meal,
even if a little stiff.
If already after the rigor, the meats been aged and tenderizing.
Skin, gut and butcher, then salt water cleanse.
Pick off any unwelcomed crawling friends.
Boil well then throw it on the grill, when it sizzles, RKT gets a
mighty thrill.

White line gourmet, chef of the blacktop, fully appreciates
there's no butcher bill.
Is it Bourbon baste, Bourguignon or Road Kill Bouillabaisse
tonight?

Road kill technician keeps roads clean and safe.
Highway smorgasbord, no squished wildlife needs to go to
waste.
What's the necrophilic fascination, to collect, preserve or just
take a taste?

— *Lina Sophia Rossi*

Scents Upon A Delta Breeze

She left the window open
on those warm summer nights,
to cool her bedroom, to smell the
the scent of flowers cooling after
a long day beneath the sun.

Roses in full bloom.
Tendrils of Star Jasmine
spreading into the nearby Ivy.
The natural border of Rosemary
bushes, favored by the bees.

Night after night the
scents reach her, envelope her
as she falls asleep; distant sounds
of trains and freeway traffic mixing
with crickets and hushed voices.

Summer after summer
the patterns repeat; open window,
cool breeze, scents and sounds, right
up to the night Death dropped by;
as sermonized by her priest,

prognosticated by her doctor,
and sanctioned by Time. Death came
smelling of rotten vegetables, road kill
decay, and fresh corpses supine
upon the autopsy table.

Death came to lead her and
others away that night, their beds
emptied of all vitality, their voices
hushed, the scent of summer blooms
drifting toward the cemetery.

— *G. O. Clark*

Serra

Beneath a gibbous moon, Serra dances
to the sway of barren limbs in the wind.
The old oak comes alive to her movements,
bendng to her in communion.
Wraiths rise from their frozen graves,
align behind its ancient trunk.

Shadows twist and swirl electric
as a jazzman's spirit plays the blues,
copacetic calibrations suiting the occasion,
for the last night of October when
the spirit world belongs to her.

Howls and moans and creaking limbs,
a celebration of what was and is to come,
unnatural or hidden in the whorls of time,
ancient oak or weeping willow,
connected in the flow of life to death,
then back again, at Serra's will.

— *Marge Simon*

Skin to Scales

beneath the whitewash
a playful prickle
or determined nibble
sharp raw enamel
tooth wedged in cuticle

ripple in the sea
mysterious blur concealing identity
glorious salty sickness
scallop shark siren
some combination of the three

wiggle within the murk
primal urges stirring
blood goes green
wet warm wicked
fantasies taken to unhealthy extremes

clothing removed stitches unraveled
now rags from a distant time
aquatic aspirations
evolution now
become one with the brine

kiss blown to the harvest moon
plunge into the dark damp unknown
pressure building until
fresh-sliced gills   appear
seconds before suffocation

aphotic dreams become reality
surreal smiles sail the smooth and silent sea
men of kelp and
web-footed women
come to welcome me

home
finally

— *Chad Stroup*

Spring's Awakening

The Beast braces to face his morning reflection
squeaking the steamy mirror clean with his palm,
grown nearly accustomed to the chilling image,

And the stark lack of recognition he exhibits
at his own gaunt cheeks, piercing gaze,
the newly feral expression clapped to his lips.

A startling garland of bruises grace his throat,
tumbles down his shoulders, blooms yellow and purple,
each vibrant mark a souvenir of his Angel's kiss.

Timidly he attempts to disprove the evidence.
His fingertip presses against one tender blossom,
A brutal boutonniere lying full on the meat of his neck.

Sensation rekindles the nocturnal lesson
when he was tamed and released, domesticated
And newly demonic by this tenderness, this distress.

Passion leaps from his root, unrestrained
Like a bell-trained hound primed to begin a race,
a course this Beast only now knows how to run.

— *James Frederick Leach*

Stitches

A simple seamstress,
my needle works a taut, invisible hem,
presses and pricks a neat path
sealing wounds beneath the skin.

Deep pain leaves a nasty scar—
see that red swelling patchwork,
that anchored ache bubbled as a blister?

In the dark I work, slicing souls
with breath like a whisper of soft string,
seeking each swollen tragedy
behind a cold, stiff smile.

Buried memories arrive like packages on a doorstep,
so I unpack bruised hearts and fractured dreams,
each full of something ugly and broken to hide.

Not yet? I'll wait. Silent in the worn crevices of a heart,
wallowing in marrow, hollowing out the gut.
Hungry for every loss you swallow,
I'm here to keep you in stitches.

— *E.F. Schraeder*

The Burial Shroud

Mankind embraced hatred,
welcomed death's dark abyss.
This time the ovens spared
only the brightest and the best.

They burned teachers, preachers, pilots, doctors,
veterans, vegans, peaceniks and warmongers.
Suicidal teen idols, both blue- and white-collar,
rich athletes and the bum who just wanted a dollar.
Workaholics, alcoholics, nature photographers,
dancers, artists, prisoners, and pornographers.
Skinheads, slumlords, feminists, activists,
Muslims, Buddhists, Christians, atheists.

When the refinement was completed,
the one percent thought they had won.
Until the ashes of the ninety-nine
rose and blotted out the sun.

— *Adrian Ludens*

The Crawling Lesson

They dumped my body in the desert
the morning after the night
they took my life.

I have no legs to walk,
no arms to drag myself away,
but in death I have found,
there are other ways
to get around.

I speak to the scorpions now.
They crawl beneath me,
their many pincers and stingers
piercing my back,
lifting my remains,
and carrying me away.

At twilight a coyote
tries to pick me off.
I spit my newfound venom
into its eyes and
watch its head dissolve
into a skull and then
into dust
that floats
down to the sand.

It is midnight when we see
the lights at the edge of town,
each one of those lights the apple
of a vulture's eye.

With what remains of my mouth
I smile,

the shattered teeth falling away,
my fresh fangs
blossoming
with ichor
and hunger.

— *James Ebersole*

The Familiar

Dreams of Darkness, dreams of fire,
fire - icy to the touch, burning water,
frozen flames, etched in blackness,
yearning to be set free....

Shadow figure, sleek and svelte,
rippled ebon, honed like steel,
motionless motion, and piercing eyes,
shifting, then vanishing into darkness....

Waking dreams of awe and wonder,
images so real, yet surreal,
nocturnal mirages, sharp then fading,
to vanish once more.... only to return....

The Familiar does not fade away,
like melting castles built on sand,
the mirage itself becomes more firm,
more familiar as it nears....

As you awake to see the maw,
the sinew and blood tipped claws,
and feel the searing pain and scream,
seeing those eyes, inches away, gleam....
malefic eyes of ice and fire.

— *Richard Groller*

The Length of His Spine

For twenty-nine and a half days
she paces the length of his spine,

claws clacking on vertebrae stacked
like blocks, while the moon shrinks
and then finally blossoms into a
dull white flower. She aches for even

the briefest sip of fresh air—the gentle
kiss of a breeze—but it's the loneliness
that spoils her blood. From behind
the filmy window of his eyes, she longs

to embrace this pack of potential brothers,
sisters, and lovers—to kiss them and
sing with them songs of elation and
release. Maddened by solitude, she

throws herself against the bars of his
bone prison. She gnaws at the hard brick

of his muscles until Moon yawns wide
and Sun snuggles into Earth. Her

growl saws through his screams. She
paws and pushes and digs into his face

until she wears him like a mask,
blood dripping from her muzzle smile.
In a frenzy, she prowls for her friends,
the mates he would hide from her. She

embraces them, claws tearing their
flesh like butterfly wings. She kisses, teeth

ripping their smiles and tongue tasting
the warm drumbeat secreted within. And

as they shriek with bliss beneath the
full manic weight of her fellowship,
she tilts her head and howls with them a
song of joy and of love and of how

for twenty-nine and a half days
she paces the length of his spine.

— Rob E. Boley

The Oak Tree's Shade

I am a ghost,
a warped shadow forming a blackened stump.
Once great;
the oldest and largest,
revered as sacred.

Clouds roll over scorched lands.
coal-blackness seeps in.
Breezes are furnace-hot,
licking gnarled splinters
which were once limbs.

So little left—
don't despair—
weep for those who once were.
Twenty centuries of children's laughter
echo through my genius.

Once a temple, heart of the village,
I became a gallows for the condemned,
and then an object of sterile beauty.
My soul could only surge forth
when giving solace to the innocent.

I am now a ghost,
a warped shadow forming a blackened stump.
Fulfillment drew from healing and feeding
but a child's awe gave me joy…

until the heat and flames took them all away.

— *Gerry Huntman*

The Orb

Some nights the dream returns to me
of something that I think occurred
far south of the Labrador sea
where northern lights have rarely stirred.

My brother and I took a walk,
restless upon a summer lark
when something offshore made us balk,
a welling in the endless dark.

An odd and glistening black orb,
much larger than our father's truck,
a sight our minds could not absorb
passing so close we had to duck.

It hovered for an endless breath
regarding us as we did it,
expressing neither life nor death
across a countenance moonlit.

I sensed that it was powerful
like some great beast caught in a lull
well fed and not concerned with us
seeking something more seminal.

Then as quickly as it was born
it dove into the murky night
ascending towards Taurus's horn
like some now tardy acolyte.

We left that strange stygian cliff
and never ever spoke of it.

— *Michael H. Hanson*

The Parasite

We are one, joined together in harmony

I touch you and you quiver with joy
My skin crawls in disgust, revulsion fills me

The bond between us is so magnificent
I want to die; I want this to end

I can't imagine a life without you
I want you gone; I hate this life

Your form fills me with happiness
I get lost just contemplating your beauty
I can only pray for this nightmare to end

When I feel you move, it is a communion of spirit
Your very existence repels me, I want to scream

Your flesh is soft, like rose petals in spring
I breathe your essence, apple and honey
You are a blight in the eyes of God

You are perfection personified, magnificent
You are the lowest of lows, vermin

The thought of losing you makes me weep
The thought of you dying makes me laugh

With our bodies joined, I am complete

I wish our symbiosis could go on forever
I dream of the day I am free of you
The day I finally hatch and fly away

— JG Faherty

The Prehistoric Garden

When we arrived at the new dwelling,
The foliage was already so beautiful and totally overgrown
Around the tiled pathways and huge corner blocks of cracked
cement.
I must admit I was a bit surprised
When barrel-shaped, chest-high palms spread sword-like angular
branches
As giant corncob appendages burst up from their honeycombed
centers
Spewing blade-like kernels everywhere.

At dusk and just before dawn, vibrant **PSYCHEDELIC**-colored
moths
The size of small bats flap webbed, reptilian wings as they
swarm.
Their extra-long antennae undulate
Like squid tentacles in deep waters
And I think I can see rows of minute dagger-shaped teeth
As their chitinous bodies suddenly collide,
Bouncing off the plexiglass floor-to-ceiling windows.

Feral parrots (I shit you not) as big as vultures
Circle in mated pairs high above the backyard.
Sometimes, their huge frames rest effortlessly on sagging power
lines
Not so high above or on broken pieces of the neighbor's fence
closer still.

In the corner of the living room,
An enormous silverfish
Crawls out of the wall on the white ceramic floor,
Glittery scales and caudal filaments twitching.
Thick centipede-like legs scurrying
With far too many sets of tiny snapping claws.

In the backyard, an ocean of giant ferns grows as thick as forest oaks.
Softball-sized spiders spin wide, sticky webs
In the sprawling arched corners
High above the driven pillars.
But the shimmering, winged spider I saw
Crawl out of the fanged, blood-glistening bloom
Scared me more because it flew away before
I could get a really good look at its human face.

— *Chad Hensley*

The Resurrection of Snow

There once was a lonely prince
who twitched like a dying fly.
He blamed his incessant trembles
on the chilling lips of Snow.

Her hair is as black as a raven's death.
Her lips are painted with blood.
Her skin is as pale as bone bleached white
But she's the only one I've loved.

He found her, the corpse of an angel
diminishing in a coffin of glass—
soaked in the light of a waning moon
lay the soft-sleeping, departed Snow.

He knelt and kissed her there
hoping to revive her with True Love.
Her eyelids fluttered, the princess stirred
to hear him pledge his life to her.

His eyes flashed with a fevered light
and his cheeks glowed fresh and sanguine.
The princess could feel the heated mad beats
of his captured, infatuated heart.

One long kiss, sharply sweet, he remembers
and he felt his sentiment ebb
as his pulse slowed and his brow grew cold
from the chilling lips of Snow.

Her hair is as black as a raven's death.
Her lips are painted with blood.
Her skin is as pale as bone bleached white

But she's the only one I've loved.

Now the lonely prince simply wastes
caught in torment—True Love's purgatory—
with no hopes to ascend from perdition
because he dared taste the cold lips of Snow.

— Angela Yuriko Smith

The Square Root of Dying

How large the darkness is,
that cold empty sphere
haunting us, waiting for us,
surrounding us like regret
or the scent of our fear.

Is it half its radius
or twice its diameter—
three times or a
hundred times pi,
this circle of despair
and loneliness?

It is too small to be seen
too large to be calculated
or even imagined.
Death's vortex
is always hungry,
drawing us deep into
its dark equation.

— *Lisa Lepovetsky*

The Tanzler Meditations: On Preserving the Corpse

Could I contain you, remain with you,
as Carl Tanzler did
with his Cuban-American beauty?
Entombed
and forever building artifice
to keep substance
from returning to shell
and shell to earth.
Ashes, as we all are.
Can I arrest the passage of time,
which has no concern
for human machinations
sane, morbid or otherwise?
The second hand ticks on,
a relentless soldier
marching ceaselessly
towards endings.
The grains of sand
ever slipping through the hourglass
and her skeletal fingers – pointing, judging.
Is there art in our breath or our structure –
bone, muscle, ligament, sinew, flesh?
We are born with the desire
to capture,
to reinvigorate,
but what is it we seek to arrest:
our own mortality
through the preservation of theirs?
Of hers? Of yours?
I only have words for dying
but I understand the Count's necessity
for the illusion of life
even in the utter absence of it.

— *Monica S. Kuebler*

The Thing that Ate You

After you died
the thing that ate you
clawed its way into my mouth
I tried to scream it out
but it made me a garter snake
and went only one way
down the hatch
I tried to close my throat
but it smothered my screams
kindly now now
and rested a minute at my clavicle
then down into my lungs
and I can scream
as loud as the furies
and it feeds on the scream
delicious oh thank you
dining on my endothelium at twilight
resting a dull hour, then
clawing inside my breast in darkness
eating
growing and no doubt
breeding

— *Mary A. Turzillo*

They May Not Tell Tales, but They Do Sing Songs

Seventeen victims
Right legs cut open with surgical precision, tibias gone
Sixteen failures
Sixteen women he could have saved
If he'd been smarter, luckier, more driven

A near miss
Their man slipped out through a hidden door
He was the one who found it balanced atop the doorframe
A flute
The color of scrimshaw in a museum he'd visited as a child

Bagged and tagged
Waiting for forensics to confirm which victim it came from
Mindy Morgan? Tricia White? Clementine O'Donnell?
Which of his sixteen failures?

Standing in the evidence room at 3 a.m.
He holds the flute
His fingers dance, skitter over smooth bone, turning it end over
end like a baton
"Where is he?" the inspector asks, and, "Who's next?"
Places his lips against the mouthpiece
A note like wind through the trees on a moonless night fills the
room
Mindy speaks.

— *Nina Shepardson*

This Is Only the Beginning

The claws of his voice scraped across my brain, rending
my thoughts indecipherable. It was a scream I may never
understand. It was a scream I can never forget.

From a dead sleep he woke shrieking.

With eyes as big as silver dollars, he stared
at an invisible something beside our bed. Trembling
and stiff, his stare never wavered as I
cradled him in my arms.

He screamed.
He pointed.
He shuddered with dread.
Then I asked him, "What do you see?"

At the age of two words are few, so he answered
with only a gesture. He raised his hands,
mimicked claws, and his lips curled back
like a rabid dog's blood-thirsty growl.

He then recoiled, curled against my chest
and cried and shook and stared.
I told him, "You are safe.
I'll always protect you."

I then waved my arm in the empty
space beside our bed where
his fearful eyes remained riveted.
Black wispy orbs scattered about and flew
throughout the bedroom. Slowly they
vanished, as my boy let out
a long, deep sigh. His muscles relaxed
and his eyes soon closed, and I laid

him down beside me. I rested my head
upon my pillow, as I watched
my boy sleep soundly. Just as I
dared to close my eyes, a hot breath
blew down the back of my neck and I heard
an unknown, guttural voice whisper,
This is only the beginning.

— *Renee Young DeCamillis*

Undercurrents

A man enters the world, covered with pinpoint bubbles clinging
valiantly to his skin.
Slow motion hair billowing outwards, a blossoming crown.
A jerking puppet, a harlequin,
      becomes regal
           and elegant in the undercurrents.

Taste becomes more sensitive and pervasive. Salt and copper.
Fish and shell.
Sound fades as the beating subsides.
Gravity plucks and pressures,
Colors fade to green, to black,
giving way to the pull of the undercurrents.

Tempted and lulled from the wooden islands, taken by choirs, by
solos.
Joyful at first, fury and terror at the last.
Caressing limbs reach toward the stars
      to guide; longing, enveloping, welcoming
           by those that live in the undercurrents.

— *Guy Anthony De Marco*

Unravel

At night

I want to be the spider
that crawls into the hair
spread across your pillow
like an inky dream.

I think
if I could just
taste your nightmares
I could spin them
into something sweet;

I could reweave them
into something softer.

I want to nest
into the silken warmth
so like my home,

burrow down to the roots

unwelcome
unbelonging
unnoticed

but nevertheless,
touching your skin.

This is all I could ask.

— *Annie Neugebauer*

Where We Are In Space-Time's Shadows

Shadows move but are they in her eyes or her rooms?
Cross-cut scratches in wood where no cat has been;
What do the prints up walls, on the ceiling mean?
Wasn't there a door there before, or another way out?

Clotted thoughts confuse. Baffling mumbles echo.
Haunt is what we do to the places in our heads.
Trembling branches tap on grime-fogged windows.
Faucets drip where no sinks stand, no tub awaits stains.

She lays in a bed that found her like a stalking beast.
Its belly is soft. Warmth cocoons her. She is naked.
Comforting touches caress her bones. Her own hands moving.
Her last awareness is her skin rippling, tearing free.

She shouts at their flickering presence, their hesitant probing:

I'm as old as I've been alive.
I've existed much longer.
Each of us is second-phase
Star-spew. We reach back

Into billions of years of space-time.
Age is just a three-letter word.
Phoneme from an ape's mouth.
Age is a grunt in the dark.

I'm here. Please hear me: I'm here. Once is always.

Skeletal remains, they call her now, found alone in bed.
Her scent is dust in their nostrils, her life is a sun beam dimmed.
Lassitude coalesces. Shadows move but are they there at all?
Her sobs, her cries, her shrieks cannot be heard by the living.

— *Gene Stewart*

Wings

Angels were tamed
when god pinched their wings
tossing them to earth
dragons were pierced
by god's avenging lance
fairies were flattened into children's tales
and every aerial creature grounded

I would do it all again
pluck a feather, a scale
a leathery membrane
stitch it onto a cloak
mask my earthbound humanity
How else can we take flight
but by leaping into the void

But such lofty goals are not to be
when a diety fears my touch
lets me melt
under the sun's withering gaze

Each one kept in our orders
until we rise up
on ephemeral spirit wings
take down our self-imposed gods

— *Colleen Anderson*

Wraith

Scarcely out of light, your face
Makes of these familiar shadows
A still portrait,
Another chance for grief.

I sometimes wait all night
For the glimpse that kills.
I never believed, so nothing
Here makes sense of nothing.

I cannot stop seeing, as you
Cannot end this thing beginning
When last you went upstairs
And never came down.

— Steve Rasnic Tem

Yew Berry

Arcane skill and kitchen magic
work to craft a wild foraged pie.
Patient fingers pick juicy pulp
From deadly seed.
Hours of plucking, careful work.
Thousands of red berries prepared
By wise hands.
The digits attentive and deft become crimson--
Seeds to the left, fruit to the right.
A few mistakes could kill a man,
But experience produces
A rare and risky filling.
Flaky pastry birmmed and baked
holds the scent of summer's peak.
Dig in.
Trust me.
You've tasted nothing like this in your life.

— *Janice Leach*

Juror Biographies

David E. Cowen is the author of three books of poetry, *Sixth and Adams* (PW Press 2001), *The Madness of Empty Spaces* (Weasel Press 2014) and *The Seven Yards of Sorrow* (Weasel Press 2016). David has been published in journals in the United States, Great Britain and Australia. David was editor of the *HWA Poetry Showcase Volume III*. David is the current President and a Lifetime member of the Gulf Coast Poet's in Texas.

Lisa Morton is a six-time winner of the Bram Stoker Award®, a screenwriter, a novelist, and a Halloween expert whose work was described by the American Library Association's *Readers' Advisory Guide to Horror* as "consistently dark, unsettling, and frightening". Her most recent releases are the non-fiction books *Haunted Nights* (co-edited with Ellen Datlow) and *The Samhanach and Other Halloween Treats*. She lives in the San Fernando Valley, and can be found online at www.lisamorton.com.

Peter Adam Salomon is a member of the Society of Children's Book Writers and Illustrators, the Horror Writers Association, the Science Fiction & Fantasy Writers of America, the Science Fiction Poetry Association, the International Thriller Writers, and The Authors Guild and is represented by the Erin Murphy Literary Agency. His debut novel, *Henry Franks,* was published by Flux in 2012. His second novel, *All Those Broken Angels,* published by Flux in 2014, was nominated for the Bram Stoker Award for Superior Achievement in Young Adult fiction. Both novels have been named a "Book All Young Georgians Should Read" by The Georgia Center For The Book. His short fiction has appeared in the *Demonic Visions* series among other anthologies, and he was the featured author for *Gothic Blue Book III: The Graveyard Edition*. He was also selected as one of the Gentlemen of Horror for 2014. His poem "Electricity and Language and Me" appeared on BBC Radio 6 performed by The

Radiophonic Workshop. Eldritch Press published his first collection of poetry, *Prophets*, and his second and third poetry collections, *PseudoPsalms: Saints v. Sinners* and *PseudoPsalms: Sodom*, were published by Bizarro Pulp Press. In addition, he was the Editor for the first books of poetry released by the Horror Writers Association: *Horror Poetry Showcase Volumes I and II*. He served as a Judge for the 2006 Savannah Children's Book Festival Young Writer's Contest and for the Royal Palm Literary Awards of the Florida Writers Association. He was also a Judge for the first two Horror *Poetry Showcases* of the Horror Writers Association and has served as Chair on multiple Juries for the Bram Stoker Awards. Peter Adam Salomon lives in Naples, FL with his wife Anna and their three sons: André Logan, Joshua Kyle and Adin Jeremy.

Michael R. Collings, WHC Grand Master, is an educator, literary scholar and critic, poet, novelist, essayist, columnist, reviewer, and editor whose work over three decades has explored science fiction, fantasy, and horror, emphasizing the works of Stephen King and related writers. He has served as Guest, Special Guest, and Guest of Honor at a number of cons, professional as well as fan-oriented, including three-time Academic GoH at the World HorrorCon. He has been nominated for the Bram Stoker Award® (Horror Writers Association) three times for non-fiction and for poetry. Retired from Pepperdine University, he lives in Idaho with his wife, Judi.

Authors' Biographies

Bruce Boston is the author of more than fifty books and chapbooks. His writing has received the Bram Stoker Award, the Asimov's Readers Award, a Pushcart Prize and the Rhysling and Grandmaster Awards of the SFPA. His latest collection, *Visions of the Mutant Rain Forest*, a collaboration with fellow SFPA Grandmaster Robert Frazier, is available from Amazon and other online booksellers. www.bruceboston.com.

Clay F. Johnson is an amateur pianist, devoted animal lover, and incorrigible reader of Gothic literature and Romantic-era poetry. When he's not intensely studying the preternatural fascinations of his beloved Romantics, working on new melancholy melodies, or entertaining his monstrously ill-behaved dogs, he can be found tracing the shadows of his imagination by writing poetry or editing his ever-changing novel. Among other literary endeavors, Clay is currently working on a long poem which will complete his first poetry collection, inspired mostly by the haunting events and supposed laudanum-induced madness that occurred at the Villa Diodati during the "year without a summer" of 1816. Find out more at http://clayfjohnson.blogspot.com/ or follow him on Twitter @ClayFJohnson.

Stephanie M. Wytovich is an American poet, novelist, and essayist. Her work has been showcased in numerous anthologies such as *Gutted: Beautiful Horror Stories, Shadows Over Main Street: An Anthology of Small-Town Lovecraftian Terror, Year's Best Hardcore Horror: Volume 2, The Best Horror of the Year: Volume 8*, as well as many others. Wytovich is the Poetry Editor for Raw Dog Screaming Press, an adjunct at Western Connecticut State University and Point Park University, and a mentor with Crystal Lake Publishing. She is a member of the Science Fiction Poetry Association, an active member of the Horror Writers Association, and a graduate of Seton Hill University's MFA program for Writing Popular Fiction. Her Bram Stoker Award-winning poetry collection, *Brothel*, earned a home with Raw Dog Screaming Press alongside *Hysteria: A Collection of Madness, Mourning Jewelry*, and *An Exorcism of Angels*. Her debut novel, *The Eighth*, is published with Dark Regions Press.

Follow Wytovich at http://www.stephaniewytovich.com/ and on twitter @JustAfterSunset.

Special Mention

Alessandro Manzetti is a Bram Stoker Award-winning author, editor, and translator of horror fiction and dark poetry whose work has been published extensively in Italian, including novels, short and long fiction, poetry, essays, and collections. English publications include his poetry collections *No Mercy, Eden Underground* (Bram Stoker Award 2015 winner), *Sacrificial Nights* (with Bruce Boston, Bram Stoker Award 2016 nominee), and *Venus Intervention* (with Corrine de Winter, Bram Stoker Award 2014 nominee), and the collections *The Garden of Delight, The Massacre of the Mermaids* and *The Monster, the Bad and the Ugly* (with Paolo Di Orazio). He edited the anthology *The Beauty of Death* (Bram Stoker Award 2016 nominee). His stories and poems have appeared in Italian, USA, and UK magazines, such as *Dark Moon Digest, The Horror Zine, Disturbed Digest, Illumen, Devolution Z, Recompose, Polu Texni*, and anthologies, such as *Bones III, Rhysling Anthology, HWA Poetry Showcase vol. 3, The Beauty of Death, Best Hardcore Horror of the Year vol. 2, Mar Dulce, I Sogni del Diavolo, Danze Eretiche vol. 2, Il Buio Dentro*, and many others. He has translated works by Ramsey Campbell, Richard Laymon, Poppy Z. Brite, Edward Lee, Graham Masterton, Gary Braunbeck, Gene O'Neill, Lisa Morton, and Lucy Snyder. He is the owner and editor-in-chief of Independent Legions Publishing and is on the Horror Writers Association Board of Trustees. Website: www.battiago.com

Robert Perez is made of nightmares. He lives halfway between reality and fantasy at all times. He currently studies psychology, sociology, and creative writing at the University of Colorado Denver. His previous work "The Man Who Disappears" and "Prey" appeared in the *Horror Writers Association Poetry Showcase Volumes II* and *III*. His poetry can also be found in *Deadlights Volume I*, and *The Literary Hatchet #13* and *#14*. Follow @_TheLeader on twitter to keep up with future projects.

Ann K. Schwader's most recent poetry collection is *Dark Energies* (P'rea Press 2015). Her poems have appeared recently in *Star*Line, Spectral Realms, Weird Fiction Review, Dreams & Nightmares*, and elsewhere. She is a two-time Bram Stoker Award Finalist (for poetry collection), and a two-time Rhysling Award winner. Her Dreamwidth blog is Yaddith Times https://ankh-hpl.dreamwidth.org/. Ann lives, writes, and volunteers at her local branch library in suburban Colorado.

Marge Simon lives in Ocala, Florida and is married to Bruce Boston. Her stories have appeared *in Daily Science Fiction, The Pedestal Magazine, Morpheus Tales* and many more. She won the Strange Horizons Readers Choice Award, 2010, the Bram Stoker Award ® for Poetry, the Rhysling Award and the Grand Master Award from the Science Fiction and Fantasy Poetry Association, 2015. She has work in *Chiral Mad 3, Scary Out There,* and *You Human*. Upcoming fiction: *Chiral Mad 4* 2017, *The Beauty of Death*, 2017. www.margesimon.com.

The Poets

Colleen Anderson's 200 plus pieces of fiction and poetry have appeared in such venues as *nEvermore!, Chilling Tales, Evolve, Deadlights, OnSpec* and *Cemetery Dance*. She is a three-time

Aurora nominee (twice for poetry), Rannu place winner, and has received honorable mentions for poetry and fiction. Her past is littered with roles as a book buyer, book rep, poetry editor for Chizine's online magazine, fantasy fiction editor for Aberrant Dreams, host of the Vancouver ChiSeries, co-editor for *Tesseracts 17* and *Playground of Lost Toys*, as well as a freelance copyeditor for many years. This year sees her editing *Alice Unbound*, as well as working on collections in fiction and poetry. New poetry is showcased in *Polar Borealis, Eternal Haunted Summer, Grievous Angel* and others. Her chapbook *Ancient Tales, Grand Deaths and Past Lives* is available through Kelp Queen Press. http://kelpqueenpress.com/colleen_anderson.html.

Benjamin Blake was born in the July of 1985, and grew up in the small town of Eltham, New Zealand. He is the author of the poetry and prose collections, *A Prayer for Late October, Southpaw Nights, Reciting Shakespeare with the Dead*, and *Standing on the Threshold of Madness*, and the novel, *The Devil's Children*. Find more of his work at www.benjaminblake.com.

Rob E. Boley grew up in Enon, Ohio, a little with a big Indian mound. He later earned a B.A. and M.A. in English from Wright State University in Dayton, Ohio. He's the author of the *Scary Tales* series of dark fantasy novels featuring mash-ups of classic fairy tale characters and horror monsters. His short fiction has appeared in various publications, including *Pseudopod, Clackamas Literary Review, Best New Werewolf Tales*, and *Intersections: Six Tales of Ouija Horror*. He lives with his daughter in Dayton. In 2016, he founded Howling Unicorn Press with his partner, Megan Hart. Each morning and most nights, he enjoys making blank pages darker. You can get to know him better at www.robboley.com.

Michele Brittany is the Editor of *James Bond and Popular Culture: Essays on the Influence of the Fictional Superspy* (2014,

McFarland & Co. Publishers) and *Horror in Space: Critical Essays on a Film Subgenre* (forthcoming, McFarland & Co. Publishers) and she is currently writing her first solo non-fiction book on mummies. She is the Book Review Editor for the *Journal of Graphic Novels and Comics*, Editorials Manager for independent publisher Fanbase Press, and a member of H.P. Lovecast, a monthly podcast analyzing Lovecraftian horror stories. An active academic member of the Horror Writers Association, she is the co-chair of HWA's Ann Radcliffe Academic Conference, focused on horror studies, and she is a member of the National Coalition of Independent Scholars (NCIS)

Kenneth W. Cain is the author of the Saga of I trilogy, *United States of the Dead*, the short story collections *These Old Tales* and *Fresh Cut Tales*, and his latest *Embers: A Collection of Dark Fiction*. Early on, shows like *The Twilight Zone, The Outer Limits, Alfred Hitchcock Presents*, and *One Step Beyond* created a sense of wonder for the unknown that continues to fuel his writing. Cain resides in Chester County, Pennsylvania with his wife and two children.

Elsa M. Carruthers is a speculative fiction writer, academic, and poet. She lives in California with her family. In 2011, she earned her MFA in Creative Writing and English from Seton Hill University. Since graduating, Elsa's work has been published in several anthologies, magazines, and e-zines. Elsa is an active member of HWA, RWA, SFPA, IAFA, and the Poetry Foundation. She regularly attends writing conventions and loves meeting new people

G. O. Clark's writing has been published in *Asimov's Science Fiction, Analog, Space & Time, A Sea Of Alone: Poems For Alfred Hitchcock, The Horror Zine, Disturbed, Tales Of The Talisman, Daily SF* and more. He's the author of twelve poetry collections, most recent, *Built To Serve: Robot Poems*, 2017. His second fiction collection, *Twists & Turns*, came out in 2016. He was a Stoker Award finalist in poetry, 2011. He lives in Davis, CA. http://goclarkpoet.weebly.com/.

Renee Young DeCamillis is a dark fiction writer, but she wears many other hats. She's also a blues-rock-metal lead singer, lyricist and guitarist, as well as a horror movie reviewer. She has an MFA in Popular Fiction from the Stonecoast Graduate program, a B.A. in psychology from the University of Southern Maine, and she attended Berklee College of Music as a Music Business Major, with guitar as her principle instrument. Over the years she's been in a number of bands where she's taken on various roles, including hand percussionist. Back in the 90's she was an A&R Rep for an independent record label. At U.S.M. she was a Fiction Editor for Words & Images literary and visual art journal. The mental health field held her captive for years as a therapeutic mentor. Teacher of Creative Writing and School Rock Band are also on her list. She's also a former gravedigger; she can get rid of a body fast without leaving a trace, and she's not afraid to get her hands dirty. Renee finds that her real world bleeds into her fiction, just as her fiction bleeds into her real world. Once she writes something and then lets time pass, she often finds that the writing has bits of prophetic visions woven throughout. It's uncanny and often horrific, but that's her life. And that life resides in the deep dark woods of Southern Maine with her husband, her son, and a house full of ghosts. You can find her at phantom1333.wixsite.com/renee-young-decamillis.

Guy Anthony De Marco is a speculative fiction author; a Graphic Novel Bram Stoker Award® finalist; winner of the HWA Silver Hammer Award; a disabled US Navy veteran, a prolific short story and flash fiction crafter; a novelist; an invisible man with superhero powers; a game writer; and a coffee addict. One of these is false. A writer since 1977, Guy is a member of the following organizations: SFWA, WWA, SFPA, IAMTW, ASCAP, MWG, HWA. He hopes to collect the rest of the letters of the alphabet one day. Additional information can be found on Wikipedia and GuyAnthonyDeMarco.com.

James Ebersole holds an MA in creative writing from Edinburgh Napier University. His work has previously appeared in *HWA Poetry Showcase Volume I*, as well as *Folk Horror Revival: Corpse Roads, Richmond Macabre, Werkloos*, and *Broken Worlds*.

Leadie Jo Flowers Unable to accept things for what everyone says they are, Leadie Jo Flowers tends to search out strange and mysterious people, places, and things through travel. Currently an expatriate in Moscow, Russia, she puts a little bit of fear into her Russian students, as well as some other misfits that occupy the planet, or any other planet for that matter. Since being introduced to Pittsburgh's *Science Fiction Theater* and *Chiller Theater* as a child, she has spent much time sifting through films, books, and storytellers that have spent their time attempting to stop a person's heart with fear alone. This fear can be as subtle as society's beliefs or the invasion of beings and sciences unknown to us. When combined with the psychology of twisted minds, finding the fear button in others becomes even more exciting. Perhaps this love of fear and frightening others is the reason she lives with two quirky cats in an old block building where many have lived and died. Her hobby is visiting cemeteries to understand past lives through their tombstones. She soaks up the cultures and stories from around the world as a means of creating new tales that challenge the psyche. When she's not enjoying her passion for writing, she practices her second love, teaching English to foreigners with her B.A. from Stetson University. Her M.F.A. in Writing Popular Fiction from Seton Hill University has granted her the opportunity to introduce readers to her realm of the world of fiction.

JG Faherty is a life-long resident of New York's haunted Hudson Valley. JG has been a finalist for both the Bram Stoker Award® (*The Cure, Ghosts of Coronado Bay*) and ITW Thriller Award (*The Burning Time*), and he is the author of 5 novels, 9 novellas, and more than 50 short stories. He writes adult and YA

horror, science fiction, paranormal romance, and urban fantasy. Follow him at
www.twitter.com/jgfaherty,
www.facebook.com/jgfaherty,
www.jgfaherty.com, and
http://jgfaherty-blog.blogspot.com/.

K. S. Forman is a writer and editor. He teaches English Composition at Weber State University to earn date night money. He graduated from the Jack Kerouac School of Disembodied Poetics at Naropa University with a Master of Fine Arts degree in creative writing. His work has appeared in several anthologies, most recently *Morpheus Tales: The Best Weird Fiction Volume 6*. He makes his home in the Rocky Mountains.

Kerri-Leigh Grady is a graduate of Seton Hill University's MFA program and holds a BS in computer science. She's a nerd with an unnatural love of dark humor, gadgets, chickpeas, animals (not that kind of unnatural), cross-choking her friends, goofy ghost investigation shows (especially when someone's screaming like a five-year-old), archery, and silversmithing. This week, she lives in Hawaii.

Richard Groller is an author of fiction and non-fiction. He is co-author of *The Warrior's Edge* (with Janet Morris and COL John Alexander), and a contributing author to *The American Warrior* (Janet and Chris Morris, Eds.). Nominated for Military Intelligence Professional Writer of the Year in 1986, he has published numerous historical and technical articles in such venues as *Military Intelligence, The Field Artillery Journal, Guns and Ammo*, and the *Journal of Electronic Defense*. A member of SFWA and HWA, Rich has been published in 6 volumes of the *Heroes in Hell* shared universe anthology as well as the horror anthology *What Scares the Boogey Man?* from Perseid Press. He has short stories in 3 volumes of the *Sha'Daa: Tales of the Apocalypse* shared universe anthology, from Moondream Press, and in two volumes of the *Night Chills* horror anthologies from Iron Clad Press. He is the editor of *The Book of Night*, an illustrated book of macabre poetry from Copper Dog publishing, and was published in *HWA Poetry Showcase Volume III*.

Michael Hanson has three collections of poetry in print: *Autumn Blush* and *Jubilant Whispers* (published by Racket River Press, an imprint of Copper Dog Publishing [CDP]) and *Dark Parchments: Midnight Curses and Verses* (published by MoonDream Press [CDP]). Michael is presently compiling his fourth and fifth poetic anthologies: *The Great Soap Rebellion* (an illustrated collection of poems for children to be published by Pumpkin Hill Press [CDP]), and *When the Night Owl Screams*, his second book of dark fantasy poems (to be published by MoonDream Press [CDP]). In November 2017, Michael's short story "C.H.A.D." will be appearing in the Eric S. Brown edited anthology *C.H.U.D. Lives!* and in June 2017 his short story "Rock and Road" will be appearing in the Roger Zelazny tribute anthology *Shadows and Reflections*. Michael has stories in Janet Morris's *Heroes in Hell* (HIH) anthology volumes: *Lawyers in Hell, Rogues in Hell, Dreamers in Hell, Poets in Hell, Doctors in Hell*, and the recently published *Pirates in Hell*.

Miriam H. Harrison lives in Stratford, Canada—a town of theater, swans, and a general over-abundance of charm and beauty. To make matters worse, she is also mother to the sweetest baby boy you can possibly imagine. And then there is Cujo the dachshund—yet another beacon of cuteness and joy. In spite of these challenges, she nonetheless manages to write dark fiction and poetry alongside her horror-writing husband, Kenneth Lillie. She couldn't be happier.

Lenore Hart grew up in a somewhat-haunted house in Central Florida, which influenced her taste in reading material early on. She's the author of nine books, including the novels *Waterwoman* and *The Raven's Bride*. Under the pseudonym Elisabeth Graves she writes the *Dark Florida* series, which includes *Black River* and *Devil's Key*, available in English and several foreign language editions. Two novels are optioned for film. She is also the editor of a critically-acclaimed dark fantasy anthology, *The Night Bazaar: Eleven Haunting Tales of Forbidden Wishes and Dangerous Desires*. Her short stories, poetry, memoirs, and articles have appeared in numerous journals and magazines. She's received awards, artist grants, and fellowships from the NEA and several state arts councils. Hart's work has been featured in *Poets and Writers* magazine, and on "Voice of America" radio and the PBS-TV syndicated series *Writer to Writer*. She's on the faculty of Wilkes University's graduate creative writing program in Pennsylvania, and the Ossabaw Island Writers Retreat in Georgia. She shares a Civil-War era house in coastal Virginia with novelist David Poyer, one entitled cat, and two modest peacocks.

Megan Hart writes books. Some of them use a lot of bad words, but most of the other words are okay. She can't live without music, the internet, or the ocean, but she and soda have achieved an amicable uncoupling. She can't stand the feeling of corduroy or velvet, and modern art leaves her cold. She writes a little bit of everything from horror to romance, though she's best known for writing erotic fiction that sometimes makes you cry. Find out more about her at meganhart.com, or if you really want to get crazy, follow her on Twitter at twitter.com/megan_hart and Facebook at www.facebook.com/readinbed.

Chad Hensley is a Bram Stoker Award-nominated author who had his first book of poetry *Embrace the Hideous Immaculate* published in May of 2014 from Raw Dog Screaming Press (available at the publisher's website and Amazon.com). His recent poetry appearances include *Skelos* Magazine #2 and #3, *The Audient Void* #2 and #3, *Weirdbook* #32 and #33, and the first seven volumes of *Spectral Realms* published by Hippocampus Press. Hensley's non-fiction has appeared in such praised publications as *Terrorizer, Juxtapoz, Rue Morgue, Weird Fiction Review* published by Centipede Press, and *Super7*

Magazine (where he was also contributing editor for most of the magazine) as well as the books *The Fenris Wolf #8, Apocalypse Culture 2*, and *The Darker Side: Generations of Horror*. Hensley saw several years of his writing on underground subjects as *EsoTerra: The Journal of Extreme Culture*, through Creation Books in 2011 and the French-language version was published by Camion Noir in 2014.

Gerry Huntman is a writer and publisher based in Melbourne, Australia, living with his wife and young daughter. He has sold over 50 short pieces of speculative fiction, the majority in various shades of dark. He has also sold a middle grade fantasy novel, *Guardian of the Sky Realms*.

R. J. Joseph is a Texas based writer and professor who must exorcise the demons of her imagination so they don't haunt her being. A life-long horror fan and writer of many things, she has recently discovered the joys of writing in the academic arena about two important aspects of her life: horror and black femininity. When R. J. isn't writing, teaching, or reading voraciously, she can usually be found wrangling one of various sprouts or sproutlings from her blended family of 11...along with one husband and two furry babies. R. J. can be found lurking (and occasionally even peeking out) on social media:
Twitter: @rjacksonjoseph;
Facebook: facebook.com/rhonda.jacksonjoseph;
Facebook official: fb.me/rhondajacksonjosephwriter;
Instagram: @rjacksonjoseph;
Blog: https://rjjoseph.wordpress.com/;
Email: horrorblackademic@gmail.com.

Naching T. Kassa is a wife, mother, and horror writer. She's created 17 short stories, two novellas, and co-created two children. She lives in Eastern Washington State with Dan Kassa, her husband and biggest supporter. Naching is a member of the Horror Writers Association and a contributor to the *Demonic Visions* series.

Mark Kirkbride lives in Shepperton, England. His debut novel *Satan's Fan Club* is published by Omnium Gatherum. His short stories can be found in *Under the Bed* and *Sci Phi Journal*. His poetry has appeared in the *Big Issue, the Morning Star* and the *Mirror* in the UK and in various places online.

Monica S. Kuebler is a contributing editor at *Rue Morgue* magazine, author of *Rue Morgue Library #3: Weird Stats and Morbid Facts*, co-producer of the Great Lakes Horror Company podcast, and founder of LibraryoftheDamned.com. She also writes monster stories, and has spent the last half decade serializing her young adult vampire series, which kicked off in 2012 with *Bleeder (Blood Magic, Book 1)*, at blood-magic.net. For more about Monica, visit monicaskuebler.com.

James Frederick Leach writes dark, speculative poetry, fiction & drama and he is double-plus proud of the recent book he wrote with Janice Leach titled *'Til Death: Marriage Poems* (Raw Dog Screaming Press: 2017). JFL is a contributing editor to the *DailyNightmare* website dailynightmare.com and YouTube channel which celebrates *Midwest High-brow Horror*. In his spare time, JFL paints pictures of dead things, makes masks and lurid puppets, and practices Chaos Magick... or at least that's his excuse for his supernaturally cluttered desk.

Janice Leach has edited four volumes of *Quick Shivers* from Dailynightmare.com. She is co-author along with her partner of a volume of poetry, *'Til Death: Marriage Poems* (Raw Dog Screaming Press, 2016).

Lisa Lepovetsky is widely published in both the mystery and horror genres. She has work appearing recently in *Devilfish Review* and *Bete Noire*. She received her MFA in writing from Penn State and has taught for them and the U. of Pittsburgh. She writes and produces mystery theaters under the title of "It's A Mystery!" Her most recent book of poetry is *Voices From Empty*

Rooms from Alban Press.

Adrian Ludens is the author of *Ant Farm Necropolis*, a brand new collection of stories and poems, published by A Murder of Storytellers LLC. Other recent publication appearances include: *D.O.A. III* (Blood Bound Books), *Memento Mori* (Digital Fiction Publishing), and the weird western novelette "Bottled Spirits" (Grinning Skull Press). Adrian has published poetry in *Illumen, Midwest Literary Review*, and *HWA Poetry Showcase Volume III*. Adrian is a radio announcer and is an enthusiastic fan of hockey, reading, and exploring abandoned buildings. Visit him at www.adrianludens.com or find him on Facebook.

Kathryn E. McGee has an MFA in creative writing from UC Riverside Palm Desert. Her short fiction has appeared in *Gamut Magazine* and anthologies including *Horror Library Volume 6, Cemetery Riots* and *Winter Horror Days*. She is a member of the Horror Writers Association. In her work as an architectural historian, she writes histories of old buildings and consults on development projects involving historic properties.

Eric Miller is the editor of several anthologies, including the Bram Stoker Award-nominated *Hell Comes to Hollywood* and the trucking-themed *18 Wheels of Horror* (which featured the Bram Stoker Award-winning story "Happy Joe's Rest Stop"). As a writer, Miller's horror story "The Patch" appeared in the anthology *Halloween Tales*, his short story "Culling the Herd" made the Best Horror of the Year's rec list, and he is a regular contributor to the online literary magazine *Hot Valley Writers*. His produced screenplays include *The Shadow Men, Mask Maker*, and the SyFy Channel hit *Ice Spiders*, which was said by the *Hollywood Reporter* to be "...first rate entertainment." Miller has also written a number of other scripts that are lurking in development, including *Dog Soldiers II*. He is currently editing his first novel. "I Haunt This Place" is his first horror poem, but he plans to write many more.

Annie Neugebauer is a novelist, short story author, and poet. She has work appearing in more than seventy publications, including magazines such as *Cemetery Dance, Apex*, and *Black Static*, as well as anthologies such as Bram Stoker Award finalist *The Beauty of Death* and #1 Amazon bestseller *Killing It Softly*. Annie's an active member of the Horror Writers Association and a columnist for *Writer Unboxed* and *LitReactor*. She lives in Texas with two crazy cute cats and a husband who's exceptionally well-prepared for the zombie apocalypse. You can visit her at www.AnnieNeugebauer.com for blogs, poems, organizational tools for writers, and more.

John Palisano has a pair of books with Samhain Publishing, *Dust of the Dead* and *Ghost Heart. Nerves* is available through Bad Moon. *Starlight Drive: Four Tales for Halloween* was released in time for Halloween, and his first short fiction collection *All That Withers* is available from Cycatrix press, celebrating over a decade of short story highlights. *Night of 1,000 Beasts* is due soon from Sinister Grin press. He won the Bram Stoker Award® in short fiction in 2016 for "Happy Joe's Rest Stop". More short stories have appeared in anthologies from Cemetery Dance, PS Publishing, Independent Legions, DarkFuse, Crystal Lake, Terror Tales, Lovecraft eZine, Horror Library, Bizarro Pulp, Written Backwards, Dark Continents, Big Time Books, McFarland Press, Darkscribe, Dark House, Omnium Gatherum, and more. Non-fiction pieces have appeared in *Fangoria* and *Dark Discoveries* magazines. Say 'hi' at: www.johnpalisano.com and
http://www.amazon.com/author/johnpalisano and
www.facebook.com/johnpalisano and
www.twitter.com/johnpalisano.

Joanna Parypinski's fiction and poetry have appeared or will appear in *Nightmare Magazine, Haunted Nights* edited by Ellen Datlow and Lisa Morton, *The Burning Maiden Vol. 2, Dark Moon Digest*, and NewMyths.com. She has an MFA in creative writing from Chapman University and teaches writing at

Glendale Community College, just north of Los Angeles, where she also plays the cello in the community orchestra. She is currently seeking representation for her most recent horror novel and working on the next one. Follow her at joannaparypinski.com.

Lina Sophia Rossi is a proud member of Horror Writers Association, lover of the horror genre and creative writer since childhood. She was newspaper editor in secondary school. She edited and published poetry in SUNY Stony Brook's Italian literary magazine, *VOCI*. Her poetry appears in the third and fourth volumes of *HWA Poetry Showcase*. She holds a BS in Biology and Anthropology, a DO, and is working on her MFA and forthcoming projects. She's a family physician, lives in NC with her spouse and four-legged critters. She can be found online at: https://www.facebook.com/people/Lina-Sophia-Rossi and http://linasophiarossi.doodlekit.com/

Allan Rozinski is a writer of poetry and fiction with a soft spot for horror. He has had poetry and stories published or accepted by *The Literary Hatchet, Devolution Z: The Horror Magazine, Bete Noire, Eye to the Telescope*, and the anthology *Muffled Screams I: Corner of the Eye*. He can be found on Twitter and Facebook. He is still waiting for Cthulhu to call.

E. F. Schraeder's creative work has appeared in *Four Chambers, Slink Chunk Press, Glitterwolf*, and other journals and anthologies. Schraeder has an interdisciplinary Ph.D. in the humanities and facilitates writing workshops at a public library in the rustbelt. Schraeder also serves as contributing editor at an animal advocacy webcomic and blog, CLAWtheory. Current writing projects include a novella and a new manuscript of poems. You can find more news at efschraeder.com and say hello on Facebook or Goodreads.

Nina Shepardson is a scientist who lives in New England with her husband. Her short fiction and poetry appears in over a dozen publications, including *Nightscript, The Colored Lens,* and *Electric Spec.* She also writes book reviews at ninashepardson.wordpress.com

Angela Yuriko Smith is a widely published author, poet and writing teacher/lecturer. She writes in several genres including YA dark fiction, poetry, non-fiction and children's books. Currently, she teaches creative writing at Northwest Florida State College and writes.

Gene Stewart lives in the midwest American wilderness outside Omaha, NE with his wife of 38 years and a mad scramble of triplet dogs. He has three grown sons and writes eerie, some say macabre, realism in fiction and poetry. He and his family paint abstract expressionism, and Gene plays a ferocious lead guitar for his own amusement. More about him, and samples of his work, can be found at genestewart.com/wordpress.

Chad Stroup received his MFA in Fiction from San Diego State University. His strange short stories have been featured in anthologies like *Splatterlands* and the San Diego Horror Professionals series, and his dark poetry has appeared in the first three volumes of the *HWA Poetry Showcase. Secrets of the Weird,* Stroup's debut novel, is available now from Grey Matter Press. Visit Subvertbia, a home for some of his short fiction, poetry, and reviews at http://subvertbia.blogspot.com/, and drop by his Facebook page as well. https://www.facebook.com/ChadStroupWriter.

Steve Rasnic Tem's novel *Blood Kin* (Solaris, 2014) won the Bram Stoker Award. His new novel, *UBO* (Solaris, February 2017) is a dark science fictional tale about violence and its origins, featuring such historical viewpoint characters as Jack the Ripper, Stalin, and Heinrich Himmler. He is also a past winner of the World Fantasy and British Fantasy Awards. A handbook on writing co-written with his late wife Melanie Tem—*Yours To Tell: Dialogues on the Art & Practice of Writing*—recently appeared from Apex Books. His work in poetry includes editing *The Umbral Anthology of Science Fiction Poetry* (a finalist for the Philip K. Dick Award) and his poetry collection *The Hydrocephalic Ward* (Dark Regions Press**).

Mary A. Turzillo's most recent poetry collection, *Satan's Sweethearts*, a collaboration with Marge Simon, was published this year by Weasel Press. Also just published is *Mars Girls*, from Apex, this being a sequel to her Nebula-winning novelette, "Mars Is No Place for Children." Her collection, *Lovers & Killers*, won the 2013 Elgin Award. She has been a finalist on the British Science Fiction Association, Pushcart, Stoker, Dwarf Stars and Rhysling ballots. *Sweet Poison*, her Dark Renaissance collaboration with Marge Simon, was a Stoker finalist and won the 2015 Elgin Award. She's working on another Mars novel, *A Mars Cat and His Boy*, and of course zillions of poems.

Aimee Williams has loved reading and writing for as long as she can remember. She particularly likes books and movies that hail from the genres of science fiction, fantasy, and horror. Aimee believes that the strange, frightening, and fantastic make life interesting and that horror is a much misunderstood genre. She especially draws enjoyment and inspiration from the classics of these genres. In addition to writing, she has a wonderful job as a library page, does volunteer work, sews spooky things, and engages in mental philosophical meandering in her spare time. She lives in a big house in the country, sharing it with her parents and siblings as well as multiple pets. Including her beloved pet bunny who loves to watch TV and assist Aimee with her writing.

Made in the USA
San Bernardino, CA
19 November 2017